Fries

Takeaways

KEN CATRAN

Lothian
BOOKS

Thomas C. Lothian Pty Ltd
132 Albert Road, South Melbourne, Victoria 3205
www.lothian.com.au

National Library of Australia
Cataloguing-in-publication data:

Catran, Ken
Fries.

For ages 8–12.
ISBN 0 7344 0266 X.

1. French fries - Juvenile fiction.
2. Factories - Juvenile fiction. I. Title.

A823.4

Cover illustration by Pacquita Maher
Book design by Paulene Meyer
Text illustrations by Anita Mertzlin
Printed in Australia by Griffin Press

I have changed all the names in this book, even the name of the town. But everything I wrote here, or other people wrote, actually happened. To protect the innocent as they say, and also the guilty — even though no charges were ever pressed.

Oh, yes, and I have changed the names of the brands of potatoes too. I know there's no such thing as an innocent potato, I just don't want some grower suing me because I defamed his brand or something.

And never in my life will I eat another fry.

— Paul Knox

One

It all started the day we got the news our fries factory was going to close. Bad news. In fact, total disaster because, as my mum said, 'this town lives off Visser Fries'.

But nobody realised what else would happen — all the other things that came from that. Like a terrorist still on the run. Like biting off ears for fun and profit. Like the end of the Fries Phantom and were the dead really walking?

And finally, the awful secret of the Dark Basement.

Some of it is funny and some of it is not. Well, the cops and the army didn't think so. But Mr Walker says I should write it all down while it is still fresh in my mind. He said I should get the other kids to write down the parts that affect them.

This sounds awfully like homework and it should. You see, Mr Walker is my step-dad and the school principal. Teachers are programmed to think about things like that and (putting it as nice as I can) Mr Walker has had an awful lot of programming.

I asked him where to begin and got a typically teacher answer. Begin at the beginning.

So, here goes.

I live in a very small town called Boot Creek. It's called that because, about a hundred and fifty years ago, a guy was crossing the river and got a stone in his boot. Well the stone turned out to be a nugget and the gold-rush was on.

Boot Creek went from a stretch of gravel and a few empty paddocks to a miner's town of about ten thousand people with a police station, six churches and thirty-eight hotels. Ten years later the gold ran out and the town was down to one church and one hotel and a few wooden houses.

The soil was good so some market gardeners came, and some farmers, and by 1900, the town had a police station again, a community hall and more houses. It went downhill again in a rural depression in the nineteen-thirties. Then, in 1950, Mr Visser came.

Mr Visser emigrated from Holland and started growing potatoes. They do well in our soil for some reason. But a lot of people also grew them, so selling his crop was difficult.

Then the lightning hit him.

And it did — literally. The story goes that he was riding back to his farm on one of those old iron-frame bikes in a thunderstorm. A bolt of lightning hit his bike and knocked him clear across the road into the creek.

He should have been killed. He was a tall handsome guy who looked like Arnold Schwarzenegger with a beard. The lightning turned his hair from black to white, overnight. And my grand-dad, who dived in and pulled him out, said, 'Cripes, Vissy, you were lucky not to end up like your spuds!'

You see, he'd been carrying a bag of potatoes on his bike and they were all nicely fried, just like they'd been in the oven.

There were too many for his family to

eat, even with four sons, so he handed them around the town. And they were great — so beautifully cooked that people begged for more.

Well (so the story goes), there were only two ways of doing this. He could load his bicycle with potatoes every time there was lightning — only next time he might get fried along with them — or he could go into the potato-fries business.

He chose the second. His insurance company thought it was a wise choice. So, for that matter, did his wife and kids. And from getting hit by lightning to frying chips, it was just a step.

Visser Fries ('the fries that vhizz down your throat') became famous. He was one of the first guys to make fries in the country. Of course a lot followed but nobody could make them like Visser Fries. They are still 'vhizzing' down throats everywhere.

Vizzer Fries are great. They taste delicious. There are thick fries, wedges, skinny fries. They've won awards, and shops and takeaways can't get enough.

And they were the best thing in our town since the old gold-rush. Because twenty people get work in the factory, and that keeps our little town alive.

Old Man Visser is gone now. His car went into the creek when it was flooding. They never found his body; funny to think that his headstone is over an empty grave.

Ah, just checking what I've done, I haven't mentioned the Great Potato Fight yet. Or the day it rained gravestones. I'll get to them.

So that's how it started — so the story goes. And that's why Boot Creek is still a town when all the other little gold-mining towns are just names on a map.

• • •

The trouble started one day when Mum came home from work. The Visser Fries factory is at the end of the road. It's not much of a place to look at. Mostly sheet iron, even a tin roof. A tall cabbage palm beside it and ivy up the side.

They use caustic soda there and when the wind's in the right direction — or wrong direction — the street smells a bit. Mum doesn't mind, it's the smell of money, she says. Mr Walker does, and says the same thing every time she comes in.

'Brought the smell home with you.'

Mum usually ignores him. Or gives him the finger. Today she just marched in and got herself a glass of water.

'Bad day chipping spuds?' asked Mr Walker.

My dad left years ago on some get-rich-quick scheme. He didn't — and never came back. A few years after the divorce, Mum met Mr Walker when the town was looking for a new school principal. He got the job and she got him. So I'm stuck with him. But he's not Dad, he's Mr Walker. That's the way we both like it.

Anyway, Mum doesn't answer. She drinks the water and refills her glass. She rubs her hands through her hair, so I keep my head down. Two glasses of water and a hair massage? I know the danger signs even if Mr Walker doesn't. And he should by now.

'Yes, I did have a bad day,' she said in a very level voice.

My sister Nicole was finishing a home assignment too. We looked at each other, then at the open ranch-sliders. About two seconds' running distance and we got ready.

Mum was rubbing her head again. Mr Walker closed his laptop. He's got short fair hair and big glasses, one of those people who just seem to fade into the scenery. He seems to always wear grey.

'Well, tell me about it. The Fries Phantom loose again?'

Mum is red-headed and always wears bright clothes. Today she had on baggy green shorts and a purple top. She's bright and always bounding around; you couldn't lose Mum in a crowd. It must be true that opposites attract.

'Chips 'n' All have made a takeover offer and it looks like they'll get the place.'

Mr Walker shrugs. As I said, sometimes you have to hit this guy on the head with a baseball bat. 'Is that a problem?' Then — he thinks — he gets the message. 'You mean they might downsize?'

'Downsize' being a cute way of saying people will lose their jobs.

'No, they won't downsize,' she replied in that very level voice. 'One of them was blabbing his mouth off in the hotel. They're going to close everything up, lock, stock and barrel.'

Sis and I gaped at each other. Mr Walker was a little slower because he's only been here six months. Just a little — but enough.

'There's always my salary —'

Splash! The water straight in his face. Smash! The glass on the floor and Mum yells with frustration. Storms off to her room — *slam!*

By the time Mr Walker wiped his spectacles, we were gone too.

• • •

We stopped at our back fence. It had broken down and a couple of sheep were through again. Sis is thin and brown-haired and Mum says she has an 'intense' manner. She's not bad-looking, because she looks like me. She thinks this is a drawback and has plans for plastic surgery.

'The factory closing,' she said.

'Town closing,' I replied.

'Don't say that!' she yelled and stalked off. She has a temper just like Mum and I'm lucky she's a year younger or I'd be suffering from 'battered brother' syndrome.

It was five o'clock. I decided to give Mum half an hour to cool off. Another half hour for her and Mr Walker to make their peace.

Town is about five minutes' walk. In fact, in about five minutes you can walk through town. At the end is the cemetery. In the centre of the cemetery is the headstone marking Hendrick Visser's memorial. It's a big tall slab of yellowish marble — Mum says like a huge stone fry — with inlaid brass lettering.

He loved this town and he loved his factory. What would he think now, wherever his final resting-place was?

Course, I didn't know then that the dead would walk.

. . .

And one last thing happened that afternoon. And like everything else, it didn't register at the time.

I was wandering down the street, hoping I'd run into Rick, my best mate. But his mum worked in the factory too, so I supposed he was somewhere getting over the bad news. Rick doesn't come into the early part of this story but he does later — with a bang.

The bus was pulling into town. It came through twice a day, picking up people, dropping mail and parcels. A big guy was waiting on his bike. Francis Allan Thompson doesn't have nice parents. And the first mean thing they did was give him a name whose initials spelled FAT. Maybe they didn't do it on purpose. Everyone calls him Roller because of the roll of fat under his chin. His father thought it up.

Roller is tall and big, seems to wear nothing else but sloppy long black T-shirts and baggy faded jeans. He shaves his head and always wears a black beret pulled down over his ears. He has little round spectacles and has forgotten more about computers than most of us know. He dropped out of school early and spends all his time on the Internet. He keeps budgies.

I like Roller, although most people think he's weird. He does a bit of computer work for people and spends most of his time in his basement.

Right now he was wheeling up and down on his bike, looking very frustrated.

'It has to be there!' he yelled. 'Have another look.'

'There's nothing, mate, all right?' snapped the driver. 'Now haul your fat backside out of the way, I'm backing up the bus.'

Roller's eyes goggled at the driver, his spectacles flashing. He hates remarks about his weight. But he backed off, scowling as the bus left.

'Something important, Frank?' I asked. I'm about the only one who calls him Frank.

He looked at me and his spectacles flashed blank again. 'Yeah. But you wouldn't understand.' He looked really unhappy.

'You heard about the factory closing?' I asked. 'No more work, no more fries.'

'No more fries?' he said. He seemed about to say something then laughed. 'There'll be fries all right.' And he laughed. It was a funny laugh and somehow nasty. Then he cycled off down the road.

I was saying that closing the factory would mean the end of the town.

Roller had something else in mind.

A whole new meaning to the word 'fries'.

Two

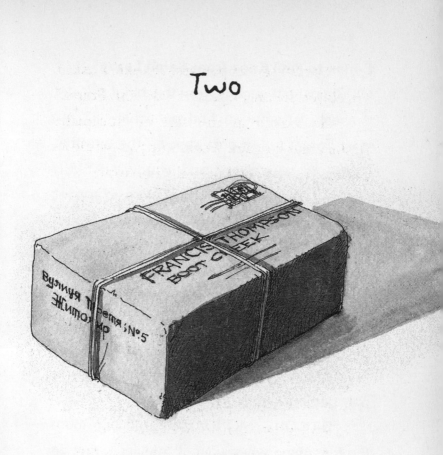

E-mail diary of Sarah Lucas (age 11) on the week of the great fries blow-up. Note: this is up to the day she left town so she will not know the events of the Dark Basement. — P.K.

E-mail to Paul Knox from Sarah Lucas:

OK Brain, I am sending you this but if it's just a sneaky attempt to find out what's in my diary, forget it. I'm only sending the bits that matter to your story and you will NEVER KNOW if Simon Hancock and I were an item at his party and you will never dare ask Simon because he would break you in half, ha ha. In return I want the answer to three questions.

Did anyone find The Exterminator?

Who was in the grave?

Is there still a price on my head?

OK, here goes, and remember you're only getting the highlights.

DAY ONE, MONDAY: I found out about the fries thing when your sister Nicole rapped on my window at about five that evening. Mum wasn't home and nor was Dad. MAJOR SHOCK! Because of Mum — well you know all about the job. So we make a big sandwich because Nicole is always hungry (and by the way, much better-looking than you) and talk about it.

Nicole (who is also smarter than you) had already sussed the whole thing. Closing the fries factory meant twenty incomes gone. Families with kids leave the town, so the school's gone. And the general store and the hotel, not to mention farm jobs — unless the Visser sons can find someone who wants a few tonnes of potatoes. With all their money, they'll be retiring.

So Mum and Dad come home and, straightaway, Nicole and me can see they know, because both are in a bad mood. They're usually fighting about something, but today they had two fights going. One they shared with each other (the fries factory closing), and one between them (what to do about it).

Nicole and me go to my room. We put on a CD but aren't really listening. It's really started to hit us both.

Nicole's mum and step-dad both work but both will lose their jobs (yes, all right, you know this, Paul), and my mum will lose hers and I don't think my dad will mind too much. Since he got laid off when the meat works closed, he's just had part-time work and wants to move to the city.

Of course Mum doesn't. To hear them carry on, you'd think he planned the fries thing himself to put her out of a job. Anyway he's already applied for a supervisor's job in the city (he says) and will know later this week. So they more or less agreed to postpone the rest of the fight until then. And neither wanted to cook, so they decided on takeaways. I can still remember Dad's parting shout — anything but fries!

Me and Nicole discussed what else it would mean. We had the big netball match coming up in two weeks and nobody can plant them like me. And Nicole had her rugby match (the one crazy thing she ever dreamed up) on Saturday. Still, nothing would happen that quickly.

We thought.

DAY TWO, TUESDAY: School was a real downer. Like a sort of national day of mourning. Even Mr Walker seemed out of it and you know what a machine he is (you've said worse things about him yourself, Paul) and our teacher, Miss Appleyard, just about had a black arm-band on.

Leila Visser is bouncing around like nothing happened. Well, she's OK, her dad cops a huge payout. And even though she's focused on the netball match with Fairmount, you might think she'd show a little class. But not Leila. No more smarts than her dad and a hide just as thick. She wants us all for netball practice after school.

William Visser was strutting around too. He's getting a new bike and a private school and he's too big to hit. I remember bumping into you, Paul, and trying to jolly you up. You're not a bad guy but you do take the troubles of the world on your head, you know.

Imogen Visser was good. Well, she's nice and her dad at least has a few smarts and is into the eco-thing. And he didn't vote for the sell-out and nor did his younger brother. But the Visser Trust will, so that's that.

As Miss Appleyard says, Visser Fries are cooked.

This is interesting stuff for me because I want to get into business. But it's also personal and that day at school was awful.

Of course things got a lot more awful after that.

After school, me and Nicole went down to the village for a shake. We sat awhile out by the shoreline because we're friends and pretty soon might never see each other again.

Chips 'n' All are going to have a town

meeting on Wednesday night and explain their plans for the factory. Maybe they will keep it working.

On the way back, the bus was pulling in. Roller was there on his bike. I just don't like this guy, there's something about the way he looks at people. Like he was looking at animals in a zoo.

Anyway, he started to hassle the bus driver and got told to shut up, his precious parcel had arrived. And for something so small, it was bloody heavy. The driver tossed it to Roller, who fumbled, and it dropped with a big thud like it was made of lead. He stuck it in his bike panniers, gave the driver the finger (got the finger back) and biked off. That guy really is the town creep.

I'm carrying on a bit, Paul, but you did say *everything*. And to mention Roller if I'd seen him and what he was doing.

For the record, I didn't see him again.

Mum and Dad not fighting that night but also not talking. At least we had a proper cooked meal.

DAY THREE, WEDNESDAY: YAAAAAAA HHHHH!!!!!! I have never heard anyone scream like that!

Wait a minute, getting ahead of myself. And listen, Paul Knox, I am not spending all night on this. Wednesday was a bad day and started off like that.

Mum and Dad were tense at breakfast. Both were going to the meeting tonight in the town hall and Dad was waiting to hear whether he had the city job.

School wasn't much better. I joined up with Nicole, who says things aren't much better at her house. Nicole's grandfather saved old man Visser when lightning threw him into the creek. Nicole said things would have been better if they'd let him get washed out to sea.

So her brother (Paul, you are up yourself

28

at times) overheard and told her she should be ashamed of herself. He said Old Man Visser would never let this happen. Nicole retorted that he was dead and this lot of Vissers didn't care. Paul yelled the vote was split and only the Family Trust decided it. And Imogen Visser overheard Nicole say that and looked pretty upset. Of course dear Paul talked to her (really, Paul, don't know what you see in that skinny pale kid, her hair sticks out like straw!), but there was a lot of tension.

And Mr Walker didn't make it better when he lectured us. This was a troubled time, and healing process, and community determination to weather the storm, and all that stuff. He's an OK principal, Paul, but he lives by the rules. I think he needs written permission from himself to be excused for the toilet. He was talking to us just before break and —

— and that was when we heard the scream!

It came from the hall and we all went about two metres in the air. Mr Walker rushed out and Nicole beat me to the door but only just. (Sorry I trod on your feet, Paul, truly was an accident) and there looking like he'd seen a ghost was Splatter-mode, otherwise known as Russell Pearson. He was rigid and looking at the big framed photo of Hendrick Visser that always hangs in the hall.

Most times it's covered with coats and Russell hasn't been there long. And if something isn't one of his CD games then he doesn't take a lot of interest. But this time he's really pale, claims he saw old Hendrick Visser standing by his open grave last night. Says that he is quite sure and he's shaking from head to toe.

It was a bit scary. Russell is such a laid-back kid, straight from the city and thinks we're all a bunch of inbred hicks — which has not made him many friends. He was so scared that Mr Walker took him home.

The Fries Phantom has the best explanation. He said to me that Old Man Visser had come back from the dead to wreak revenge on everyone who was trying to destroy his fries factory. That the Vissers who had voted for it would all die horrible gruesome deaths.

William Visser (Bill to his mates but I wasn't one) said if Old Man Visser was back from the grave then he (the Phantom) had better look out because everyone knew what he got up to. He said the Phantom would probably die by being stuffed full of fries until he exploded.

The Phantom thought this sounded cool.

Anyway I pass the cemetery on the way home, so I went in, just to have a look. I'm not scared of ghosts and anyway I'm not a Visser and I ride a pretty fast bike. (And yes, Paul, I know you were there, ducked behind a tombstone when you saw me coming.) And the ground around the Visser grave was disturbed, a little pot of flowers knocked over.

I did get a bit of a creepy feeling but only biked quick out of the cemetery because I wanted to get home and have a snack, OK?

That night we went to the town hall for the meeting and it was awful — worse than any ghost. I'd rather have a hundred ghosts haunting the place than that bunch from Chips 'n' All.

They arrived in three limos. They were all well-dressed and looked as slick as something out of a fashion magazine. First there was this woman ('anorexic fashion victim,' whispered my mum), who was a PR person. She said the company had agonised over this and would do its best with grief counsellors and even retraining programmes. (Mum yelled out, 'Train for what? There's no other business in town!')

The woman said we could look at tourism, handcrafts, even getting another industry to the town and Dad said she was lucky nobody had brought any rotten tomatoes otherwise she'd be wearing them now.

Then the Chips 'n' All guy got up. He said the decision to move north wasn't final (meaning it was, muttered Mum). That the company had the interests of the town at heart (meaning it didn't give a toss, muttered Mum), and that they had a duty to their shareholders (meaning that all they were thinking about was profit, muttered Mum).

Jon Visser, the eldest son of Old Man Visser got up then. He said they had to move on and it was better to sell the factory while it was still profitable. He said it was unfortunate for the people who worked there but the decision was made by the Visser Family Trust and so out of his hands.

Moira Burton got up then. Nobody expected her to because she's little, round and very shy and lives on her own with five cats she saved from drowning as kittens. She works in the factory, spotting for potatoes that have bad bits that need cutting out. Paul's mum says a bad potato never gets past her.

She asked the Chips 'n' All people who did they think they were. She said their shareholders made enough money. She said they all got fat salaries; just one of the BMWs outside was worth more than she could save in a lifetime.

She said it was just power and greed with them. They were hurting many lives and did not care. She said money should not rule their lives or ours. She said the factory was making enough money and what did they want more for — to stuff in their coffins and take with them when they had an early heart attack? And had they asked their shareholders? And would their shareholders like to come down and talk to us? Or could we go up and talk to them?

Silence after that. I mean she'd said just about everything and she actually made them uncomfortable a moment. Even the PR fashion victim shifted like her chair was suddenly hot. I don't know who was going to talk next, Paul, but suddenly came a clang and crash from outside.

Then another one, as everyone reacted and rushed out. Two of the BMWs had big holes in the roof or through the windscreen. And one of the Chips 'n' All guys, who was out for a cigarette, just gaped and said the stones came out of nowhere!

They were big round stones of a kind you just about only find in our area. There's a lot in the river, washed smooth by the water but these ones were painted white and they looked just like the circle of painted white rocks around Old Man Visser's grave.

That was the end of the meeting.

And an e-mail was waiting for Dad when

we got home. He got the city job. And they wanted him to start at once.

So that was the end of us in Boot Creek.

I was really going to miss the town and my friends. But suddenly it was a very scary place. First the disturbed grave then the gravestones dropping out of nowhere.

THURSDAY: We were packing the stuff we'd need and arranging for the movers. And putting the house on the market with just about no chance of selling it. So I didn't talk to anyone and didn't really want to.

FRIDAY: And what can I say about Friday except that I have never seen so many potatoes all over the place in my life.

Yes, and the local cop finding out those stones did come from Mr Visser's grave. As did the other two which landed on the roof of the fries factory and went through the roof of Cornelis Visser's truck.

SATURDAY: I've written a lot of personal

stuff in my diary that I am not telling you, Paul Knox. Saying goodbye to Nicole and my really good friends — yes, even you, Paul. Dad going on ahead, Mum and me crying when we left.

And one really rude moment. Leila Visser comes charging up and accuses me of treason!!! She says I won't be here for the netball game and I yelled back, so talk to her Dad about that. And she had the utter cheek to say that the netball team had a meeting about it and I was fined one milkshake per girl or never show my face in Boot Creek again. And if I ever played them in another team, I would leave the court on a stretcher.

We saw Leila on the way out but Mum refused to run her over.

Yes, and we lost Dad's pet ferret, The Exterminator. He'd been training it to hunt rabbits and refused to believe it was an accident. So things are still tense here and I'm in this huge urban primary school and hate it.

Let me know what happens, Paul. I think about Boot Creek every day.

SARAH

PS I like you more than Simon Hancock.

PPS E-mail from Nicole! Is it *true* the Fries Phantom has sworn never to eat another fry? What happened after I left!!!?

Three

What follows is a statement from Russell Splatter-Mode Pearson who insists on calling it a 'deposition' because his dad is a cop. I don't know much about Russell, well, I didn't until I read this. He has two

sisters who live with his mum (she and his dad are
separated and he's staying with his dad for a school
term.)

I think he said a lot more than he meant to.
Anyway I know him better now and he's not a bad
guy. — P.K.

• • •

Russell Pearson, Deposition: Dad says
this is the right expression, not 'statement',
and since I want to be a cop too, I'd better
start thinking like one. Although I want to
be a computer cop and trace massive bank-
ing scams and creeps on the Internet.

I never really liked coming here. We
had a big school in the city, lots of things
happening, a big computer room and I had
lots of friends. Now I'm stuck in this little
school with one computer and zero mates
and all the kids here think I'm strange. Well
I <u>know</u> they are.

Dad and Mum broke up last year. He was on a homicide squad and investigating murders. It sounds like a cool job but Dad got burn-out after a few years and got a transfer to country work. So he has this town and two others to look after. And this fries thing has hit him too because he says if Boot Creek goes, then so does his job. It's called 'Resource Rationalisation' and means they'll give him early retirement. That means some two-bit job as security guard or something.

So Dad was not too happy either. He likes Boot Creek and says it's a great place after the city. And he doesn't drink like he used to or wake up yelling with night-mares.

I play a lot of computer games because I just don't seem to get on with anyone. There's just this little town and the big fries factory and no crime — well almost no crime. Because there's the Fries Phantom and Dad says he would love to catch him.

I should say something about the Phantom because he's the reason I was going past the cemetery. And I don't scare easily but when I saw that photo — anyway, I'll come to that.

Dad says the Fries Phantom is the bane of his existence. I looked up 'bane' and it means basically the thing you hate the most. This may sound strange because Dad has dealt with all kinds of low-life murderers and drug-dealers. But he says the Phantom is worse than any of them because he keeps on getting away with it and nobody knows how he does it.

I have to talk about the Phantom before the cemetery thing but before I talk about the Fries Phantom, I have to talk about the fries factory. And your mum, Paul Knox, who I might say, is a lot nicer than you. I met her at the factory one Saturday when it was obvious the Phantom had been there the night before and Mr Miller, the Fries Manager, was getting at Dad for the hundredth time. And for the hundredth time, Dad was telling him he needed evidence and we all knew what the Phantom did with the evidence. He ate it.

Your mum took me around and showed me the place. It was incredible, I never knew people ate that many fries. Four tonnes of potatoes a year. They have to be harvested before April, otherwise the sugar buildup ruins them. And the factory makes about twelve thousand kilos a month.

'Eleven and a half thousand kilos with the Fries Phantom on the loose,' she said. I think she was joking.

Mr Miller doesn't joke about the Phantom, though. He is a tall guy who looks like he should be running a funeral home.

He has a face like a sad old dog and is a vegetarian, except for the fries — he never eats them.

Anyway, your mum showed me round the place and I couldn't see how anyone could get in. Just those high windows and the steel doors and padlocks. Wire mesh over the windows and a burglar alarm that would wake the dead — oops, not a nice thought when you think what happened.

Dad had sat all night in the factory sometimes. So had Mr Miller and they often went around it at night. They sometimes bumped into each other but they never bumped into the Fries Phantom.

But they always knew he'd been there because there was this big 'F.P.' arranged on the floor in fries. By then he'd eaten so many that he could afford to waste some.

And the Fries Phantom sounds like some evil, dark creature, but he's not. I couldn't believe it when I first saw him. He is skinny and small with fair hair and a freckled face. He never says much in class and lives with his dad and his step-mum, who are both eco-freaks.

They also know their civil rights backwards and won't let my dad anywhere near their son. They don't believe he steals fries and say he doesn't even eat them at home. And that he is still going through the grief process for his old grandfather who died recently. And 'until you have some evidence, officer, get off the property and don't tread in the organic radishes again.'

• • •

Sometimes Dad is away most of the night and when that happens, I take a bike ride out. I'm not supposed to, but it's nice to get away and just bike along the shore when the tide is out. Everything smells clean and salty and the water 'shushes' in a quiet way. My bike-wheels make deep marks in the sand and the water washes them out smooth.

Dad is having a tough time right now. People in the town are just starting to realise — like delayed shock — that they are headed nowhere and there is incredible bad feeling. There is even talk about torching the place and Dad takes that very seriously indeed.

It isn't helped either by the factory employing mainly women, when a lot of men are unemployed or just have part-time work, because that is called the 'Rural Down-turn'. So he's often breaking up 'domestics', too.

So I was biking along and decided to head back home. Dad sometimes calls and gets suspicious if the answer-phone is on. I was thinking about how it would be nice if he got back together with Mum. She's pleased he's not hitting the bottle any more and I think she misses him. But she thinks Boot Creek is the back end of nowhere and she's right.

So I turn for home and go up a boat ramp. There's a light there, the last light of the street, and I saw some broken glass. Somebody had chucked a bottle there so I stopped to pick it up. I rested my bike against a boatshed and picked up most of the glass. I took it around the back to put in a bin and suddenly — the Fries Phantom whizzes past on his bike. I know he lives near here. And he must know Dad's out of town because his house is by the main road, he'd have seen him drive past. So I figure the little guy's out for another snack and I can finally clear up the mystery of how he gets in. So I follow.

It's easy enough. I keep back, riding

on the path in the shadow of big hedges and trees. The Phantom sails along like he's just out for a night ride, but it's after midnight.

He comes to Visser Fries and goes on past. The town is strung out along the shoreline where Boot Creek itself empties into the sea. Past the town and the fries factory is the cemetery. Then an old church that is closed now.

I kept following the Phantom. He went past the cemetery then the old church. I biked up as far as the church and looked around. He was gone.

There was a full moon and the land is flat around there, with just a few humps of gravel where the old goldworkings were. It's all gravel and almost nothing grows there. Nowhere for even a skinny kid and his bike to hide, but the Fries Phantom was gone like the gravel had swallowed him up.

I cycled around the church but it was closed and the windows had shutters over them. Nobody used it now, it was practically derelict. It was utterly quiet and just that silver moonlight everywhere and I heard this sound.

It was a shuffling and a muttering sound. And a scraping sound like earth was being moved. It didn't sound anything like the Fries Phantom but I decided to look. I leaned my bike against the rusty old spiked iron fence that runs around the graves and went inside. The old gate squeaked and the shuffling earth-moving noise stopped.

I felt a bit spooked then.

But I suddenly thought it was the Phantom, knowing he'd been followed and trying to scare me. So I went quietly around the corner of the church, because a cop's son does not scare easily.

There was nothing around the side of

the church but a lot of the old graves. Some had tall leaning headstones and threw black shadows in the silver moonlight.

There was no sign of the Fries Phantom.

I went around, wishing I had my torch. I had seen the gravestone of Hendrick Visser when Dad showed me the place once. The brass lettering shone pale in the moonlight. And there were these big round riverstones, painted white, circling the grave.

The grave itself looked strange. Then I remembered it had lots of quartz pebbles scattered over it that shone and winked in the sun. Now they were thrown to one side and the earth was fresh, like someone had been digging there.

This crawly prickly feeling came over me, as though someone was watching me. And there was a smell, strange and musty and mouldy, and a little sound behind me. And at the same time, these long brown fingers, thin and hard as a skeleton hand, come clutching down on my shoulder. It felt like ice! So I turned around and wished I hadn't.

An old man was standing there. He had white hair and a long white beard, but his eyebrows were black over staring eyes. He was dressed in a long black coat that smelled horribly of mould. And he was thin and wrinkled and opened his mouth to show yellow teeth.

And he made a sort of 'yahhing' sound and his breath wheezed, like he was just getting used to breathing again. And I found myself backing off and he turned. His eyes seemed to glow in the moonlight so I backed a little faster. He took a step towards me and I heard his old bones click like they weren't used to movement.

I'm a cop's son and I should have just stood there and asked him questions. But what you think about doing, and what you do, are sometimes two different things. There was just him, standing about two metres tall, his hair silver in the moonlight and glaring — and me with the headstones around me.

It didn't help that I like horror movies where the rotting corpses come alive and burst out of their graves. I sort of remember standing there, then I remember being on my bike and speeding off down the street.

Then I stopped because it was crazy. I know there are no such things but I had just freaked. So I went back, staying on my bike as I circled around the cemetery. It was just as I left it but there was no old white-haired man in a black coat.

It was so weird that, when I got home, I thought I'd imagined it all. And next morning I biked past the cemetery again on the way to school. Old Man Visser's grave looked ordinary in the sunlight and all those quartz pebbles were back over it.

But it was still spooky. I had never seen Old Man Visser but the image of that spectral figure was somehow burned in my mind. And when I got to school, I hung my bag on a hook and took off my bike helmet.

Then I saw it. The framed photograph.

I'd never bothered to notice it before. But it was him, the old man by the grave, the same burning eyes. And they looked straight at me and I think I yelled. Because I backed a little as I saw the photo and some iron coathooks jabbed my shoulder like bony fingers.

So maybe I did yell a bit loudly. And Mr Walker came out and half a dozen kids behind him. And I was shaking so much he drove me home.

I didn't tell him what I'd seen. I just said I felt suddenly queer and I did. Because it's not often you see a man standing by his grave and smelling like he's been in it for about the ten years that old man Visser has been in his.

That's just about the end of my deposition.

four

UPDATE: *I have to take over the story again now because some of the parts you've already heard concerned me. And because of other things that also happened then. — P.K.*

WEDNESDAY: I know why old man Visser's grave looked OK again when Russell biked past it the next day. Because I decided to have a look at it myself after school. I asked Rick, my best mate, if he wanted to come along but he had his head buried in a book. I looked at the title. Castles! He just muttered something about being interested in knights, stuff like that. First time for everything, I suppose.

Anyway, I biked down there, just for a look. And who should I see but Mum by his graveside. She didn't look surprised, just waved to me. She explained the grave was a bit disturbed as were a couple of others. And the reason why was over in the corner.

I looked. A sheep?

She said someone had left the gate open and the sheep had wandered in. I asked how Russell could mistake a sheep for a skinny two-metre old guy in black and she said it was nerves. Just try walking into a graveyard at night and see what *my* imagination would do. In the afternoon sunlight, it all sounded clear and sensible.

I knew why Mum was here, too. She always had a soft spot for Old Man Visser, thinks he was worth all his sons put together. You see, Grand-dad fished him out of the creek and, in gratitude, he gave Mum the job as forewoman. 'Executive Team Leader' she likes to say. She was really sorry when he died, and put flowers on his grave often.

'I'm glad you're here,' she said. 'We can have a talk.'

I could have made a run for it but Mum can be pretty fast herself. And I *knew* what she was going to talk about.

There was an old stone bench by the church and we sat down. Mum said things were going to be tough. Mr Walker could probably get another job as school principal but it would be uprooting stakes here. She knew that would be difficult. But we had to pull together.

And (she said) it would help if Nicole and me stopped treating Mr Walker like he was a paying guest. Even not calling him 'Mr Walker'. OK, he was school principal but I would be going to college next year. So maybe I could call him by his first name (Stephen) or even Dad?

I shook my head at that. No way was I calling him Dad. Even though my dad had been away for a few years (about three postcards in that time), he was still Dad. I knew Nicole felt the same.

'Mr Walker's so stiff,' I said. 'He never makes jokes and living with a principal's like bringing school home. And he's always like — like nothing ever happened to him.'

'He lived with his mother till he was thirty,' said Mum.

Yeah. Right. At least my dad took risks,

even if they didn't get him anywhere. The bravest thing Mr Walker ever did was sharpen pencils. I said this to Mum.

She just looked at me. Did my dad ever remember a birthday? When did you get your last Christmas present? When did he ask how you were getting on? Or send any money? If all that makes a great dad then he's A-1. And that Mr Walker didn't have to take on a divorcee with two kids but he did.

She stops and sighs. So, at least will I try? I nod. We've had this conversation before.

We got up to go and something flashed in the afternoon sunlight. I went over to pick it up. It was an old gold watch! It had funny lettering on it; I was looking when Mum's hand came down on mine.

'Belongs to Mr Miller,' she said. 'I'll see he gets it.'

She slips it in her pocket and makes home noises. I make 'want a shake first' noises and bike off. When I look back, she's still by Old Man Visser's grave. I'm not silly. And my Mum doesn't think I'm silly. And I am smarter than she thinks. Mr Miller wears a cheap plastic watch, he never owned a gold one. And Mr Miller hated old man Visser for some reason — didn't even go to the funeral. So he would hardly go near the memorial.

And I had seen that watch somewhere before, or at least one like it. Only it was painted when I saw it.

Our town museum is the old courthouse that's never used now. It's full of old photos, a plough, stuffed animals and birds — even a zebra, which shows the crazy things people bring home from overseas. And in the hallway is a big oil-painting of the guy who donated enough to make the museum possible.

Old Man Visser.

I *knew* I'd seen that watch somewhere before. We all had to do an essay on this place because Mr Walker wanted us interested in the history of the town. Old Man Visser, white-haired and a long white beard — just like the guy Russell saw by the grave. He had on a black suit and waistcoat. On the waist-coat was a gold watch and chain.

It was just like the gold watch I found. I looked closer.

The artist had even painted the funny-lettering. The initials 'H' and 'V'. Hendrick Visser.

I knew about that watch because Mum had told me. It was about a hundred and fifty years old and belonged to the first Hendrick Visser. Old Man Visser had brought it out with him from Holland and it sounded the chimes for every hour. But his will said the watch should be buried with him.

And since my mum wasn't a grave-robber (you can't rob an empty grave), there was something wrong.

So who was standing by his grave? Not a sheep, I thought. Maybe someone pretending to be him? But why? Could anyone return from the grave? I shivered.

I shivered because it was spooky standing there in the shadows. And I was upset because Mum knew more than she was telling. A scam to scare the Visser sons? That seemed more likely so I thought I'd better let her get on with it. And ask her about the watch later.

I turned to go, and heard a noise from the other room. I looked in and there was Roller. Black T-shirt, baggy jeans, beret. I'd never seen him in the museum before.

Now he was standing in front of a big long photo of the early town; one of those joined-up panorama ones, when it was three times the size it is now. He was looking at it intently, hands to sides, his nose almost touching the glass.

'Hi, Frank,' I said.

He jumped and turned around quickly. It's a funny thing about Roller, he never seems to show any emotion. Maybe because the light is always reflecting off those thick little spectacles he wears — you can never see his eyes.

People don't like Roller, but I do. His dad's a top wheel in some computer outfit he runs from home. His mum — step-mum actually, his real mum is dead — writes books about good living and flits off to the city once a month to do a television show. Roller's on his own a lot.

There was this time my pet budgie was sick with some rare bird disease. The vet gave up on it but Roller didn't. He just turned up one night and asked for it. I got it back a week later, left on the doorstep in a little travelling cage, as bright as ever. I was eight then and had taught the bird to say 'hello Paul', so it really meant something.

'Want a shake?' I asked.

'No.'

'The town's changed a lot since that picture, hasn't it?' I said.

'Things do change,' he said.

Then he just walked past me to the entrance. He stopped and turned around. 'Paul, how far is it to Davistown?'

Our nearest big town. 'About sixty Ks.'

'No, how long, by bike? You ever done it by bike?'

I bet Roller hasn't, not with his weight. 'Ah — three to four hours, Frank. Why?'

'Just wondering.'

And he was gone. I went out a moment later and he was nowhere in sight.

I got back on my bike and went down to the cemetery again. It looked normal now, except for the line of big white-painted rocks around the grave. They were spaced evenly and I counted the deep marks of the missing stones. Four of them.

Two had been used so far.

I looked around but there was nothing else.

NOTE: *And listen Sarah Lucas, I did see you bike past and I did not duck behind the headstone, I was doing up my shoe. And if you get to read this, I do miss you. Even though you are a bit like Nicole and she is the biggest pain in the backside ever.*

. . .

When I got home, Mum was getting dinner ready. Mr Walker often helps, but she had shooed him out of the kitchen. It's always difficult talking to him. I mean, he never asks how was my day at school — because he knows. And I can't moan about my teachers, because he's one. Or even moan about the other kids, because he's principal. And anyway I had a lot to think about.

Including what my mum was up to.

And to make things really bad, there's this screech and Nicole bounds in. She's just like Mum, the way she does that. Both fists up in the air, her face alight.

'I am the greatest, I truly am. I am awesome! I am the most clever, wonderful, person ever. I am full of incredible vision and power.'

'You're full of something,' says Mum.

'What are you being so affirmative about, Nicole?' asks Mr Walker, which is exactly the thing he would ask.

Nicole tells him and us at the top of her voice. You see Nicole doesn't play basketball, she wants to play rugby; she's got together this mixed-gender team (Mr Walker's expression, not mine) to play the next small town — Hadley, our deadly rivals and famous only for the brussel sprouts they grow. Yuk!

Nicole heard Eric the Ear-biter was touring around. Eric is a top rugby player and nearly always manages to half-kill someone during a game. His favourite trick is to bite ears and quite a lot of other rugby players look pretty well-chewed.

Of course Eric has been fined and suspended so often that he spends more time off the field than on it. But right now he's touring on what Mum called a 'PR Makeover'. And Nicole has been e-mailing frantically to get him to stop at our school.

'Wonderful, wonderful, he's coming tomorrow,' she yells. 'We can learn more from him in half an hour than —'

She stops talking and that is quite difficult for Nicole. Maybe it had something to do with the bit of sliced tomato Mum chucked at her — or remembering that Mr Walker is the rugby coach. Of course, he just smiles.

'It'll be a good experience for you, Nicole,' he says.

The match is on Saturday. I even felt a tiny bit sorry for him. He had spent a lot of time with the team. 'All Eric can teach you is how to bite people's ears off,' I said.

'Better hang onto yours then,' she retorted and went to her room. Nicole always has the last word.

In the kitchen, Mum was grating carrots. I thought about the cemetery thing and wondered what was going on. I even thought for a moment about Roller and his question. But Roller was strange anyway, and my mum wasn't.

Something was going on.

Then I noticed something else. It was only a little thing, but like a lot of little things it went on to something awesome. Mr Walker had brought out a brown leather satchel with one of those small combination locks. I think he kept his important stuff in there, passport, teacher's licence, etc. He was sorting through it, maybe he thought he might need his CV soon.

Anyway, there was this bundle of news clippings and the rubber-band snapped. They went all over the floor and with my 'be-nice-to-Mr-Walker' lecture in mind, I bent to help him pick them up.

'No!' he snapped. Then recovered himself and said, 'No thanks, Paul, I can handle them.'

He stuffed them back into the satchel and closed it. And he spun the combination to lock it.

five

This is Jimmy Logan's story, otherwise the Fries Phantom, twelve years old and a local legend. He doesn't know the full story, nobody does except me and a few others. I like the Phantom but Mum disapproves of him — for obvious reasons. Anyway, here goes. He has insisted on the subtitle. — P.K.

The Fries Phantom and the Land of Syb

Hello. Paul said just tell this as it all happened. He said begin at the beginning but I'm not sure where it begins. I like Boot Creek and I like being called the Fries Phantom because it means everyone knows who I am. My fame has spread to the other towns.

Now it's over, I suppose it's OK to say everything.

It really started with my dad. He and Mum divorced, you see, because they married young and she wanted to see the world. He found someone else, and I stayed with him. I still see lots of Mum and she's really cool but she runs this big travel agency now and jet-sets all around the world. She has a big apartment and when I stay with her, it's like going to a different world.

Dad is a greenie. He's sort of very strict about it (Mum says fanatical) and we grow all our own food. A few years ago, he announced we would all be vegans. It sounded cool at the time, like something from outer space but means 'vegetarian' so we don't eat meat of any sort.

Well, fries aren't meat but Dad doesn't like fast food anyway. And hamburgers or fried chicken — he said there's so much chemical stuff in them that you should be dead before you have time to lick your fingers.

Mum lets me eat them when I go to see her. Dad says she has forgotten her early days on the commune where they met. He says she is a 'sybarite' now.

I looked up 'sybarite' once. It means someone who likes luxury and self-indulgence. I'd love to live in the land of Syb because I bet you could get whatever you wanted, and what I like are fries.

Dad grows potatoes and we have fries at home. But there's something about take-away fries. Yeah, says Dad, chemicals in the seasoning. But I just love them. I'm a fries junkie. I could eat them all day and even dream about them.

In my land of Syb, there would be fries everywhere. Fries in big tubs for everyone to help themselves. Fries delivered on request and fries-dispensers. And you could eat all you want and still be hungry. I mean chocolate, ice-cream and stuff like that are OK but fries are magic, all by themselves.

So living near a fries factory was always hard. I loved hanging around the factory and when the cooking smell came out, I could close my eyes and be in the Land of Syb. I didn't even mind the caustic smell because it was part of fries.

The women who worked there were OK, too. But the one person I didn't like was Mr Miller, the manager.

Mr Miller looked like a tall sad two-legged dog. Once I went into the fries factory and asked for a job. I said he could pay me in fries only not tell my Dad. The women laughed. Mr Miller chased me out.

And just to show how mean he is, he *did* phone my Dad and I got the lecture to end all lectures and a huge book to read on toxic waste in our food. It didn't put me off fries but I never wanted to read another book.

So that's how things went on for a while. I felt like a cat outside a mouse-farm or a vampire outside a blood bank. I even thought about digging a tunnel, but we are a kilometre away and it would have taken years. And if I ever got near the factory, it seemed like Mr Miller was always watching out for me.

The really mean part about it was William Visser. He's one of those kids who think they own the world. Just because his dad's got big bucks and mine just gets by. And he had fries every day at school, and he ate them in front of me. He even waved them at me before popping them into his mouth. All his mates did the same.

Mr Walker caught him doing it. He made William write a two-hundred word essay on the history of potatoes. I like Mr Walker, he's fair and he takes an interest in things. He's talked to me a few times about my fries thing but I don't mind that; even like it a bit.

And it was Mr Walker who got me into the factory, although he will never know it.

He took us to the town museum because we all had to do an assignment on town history. OK, so we were looking through the place and in one corner is this map. It was from the nineteen-thirties and showed how big the town was. Visser Fries wasn't built then so I wasn't interested.

Then I noticed something.

The map showed the main street, and the end bit, marked 'Block 22' was marked Miller and Sons, Shingle Haulage. That was the fries factory bit and under it was a red line. The line went under the church behind it and ended by the shore. It was marked, 'proposed new storm drain direction'.

What if they built one and never used it?

What if it was still there?

Maybe I could get in. Mountains of golden fries waiting for me like pirate treasure. But funnily enough I didn't think past what would happen if I got inside. Whether I would eat any fries — because I'm not a thief.

I just wanted to do it!

That evening.

. . .

Dad was away, delivering stuff to the Davistown markets. His partner, Jewel-Feather (yes, that's really what she calls herself) was there but she always did meditation after dinner. She called it 'communing with earth-force'.

The earth-force always kept her busy for at least an hour. I grabbed a torch and biked off down the street so fast I didn't even look at the fries factory. Past the old church and skidding my bike down the bank.

It was there. Under a lot of creeper and that sticky-vine stuff. I put my hand through and felt a rusty old chain that snapped when I pulled on it. I left my bike by the bank and pushed my way through. There was a bit of overhang there and an old concrete door lintel. A wooden door supposed to be chained shut. I could easily force it open.

It was dark inside and smelled damp. I flashed the torch ahead and started going down. I'm not tall but had to bend my head or get it knocked on concrete beams that had been set along the tunnel. The sides were rough rock that looked like they'd been worked with a pick.

A lot later, I found it was an old miner's

tunnel; some guy chasing a seam of quartz that he hoped would turn into gold. Then years ago they were going to turn it into the storm-drain but that all ended when the town got smaller. So they put in a strong door and forgot about it. That was about fifty years ago.

Now I had found it. And it led under the church (a bit spooky passing the cemetery and knowing there were bodies near me in the ground) and straight for the factory.

I could not believe it! But it was true!

I crawled until the tunnel ended in a wall of bricks. They were damaged and cracked, though — maybe from stuff carried down in the floods. The cement between them was old and crumbly and I could pull them out.

On the other side, just like the map said, was the new storm drain. It was empty now and dry, and I could crawl along until I reached a wire-mesh grille. The drain under that was wet.

I knew where that led to!

Success!

The wire-mesh grille was detachable, so I climbed up. There were little hand-holds in the pipe and I soon got to ground level. And there, through another mesh, was the factory.

I felt like a bank robber who had just cracked the biggest bank in the world.

There was just one catch. Well, two catches.

One was that the mesh grille leading in wouldn't open from this side. The other was that all the fries were stuck in a freezer each night; so my dreams of mountains of golden fries were just that. Dreams.

Then I looked up. The shaft still went up, maybe becoming an air vent. Anyway, I went up too, and it did a sharp turn into a square little metal passage. I could just squeeze into it and pushed the torch ahead of me.

The first grille I came to was just over the

big machine that cuts the potatoes into fries. I liked fries but I didn't want to be cut up like them so I kept going. The second grille had a light below it, so I wriggled up as quietly as I could and looked down.

You will not believe what I saw!

Mr Miller was there. It looked like his office and he had some big plastic containers of fries. They were white uncooked ones and he was shovelling them into big plastic bags. I flattened myself over the grille and looked down — what was he doing?

In the land of Syb, there are lakes of fries where you can just swim and dive through them — with your mouth open, of course. I knew it was all just dreams and I was sorta growing out of them — then they came true.

The grille suddenly gave way and I crashed through, headfirst, onto the table. Bags of fries squished and scattered under me — and there I was, lying on this bed of fries and looking up into the face of my worst enemy.

. . .

Mr Miller pulled me off the table. He spluttered and waved his arms around and shouted. He was going to call my dad, call the town cop; get out a court order against me.

Meantime I was a bit winded and looking around. What was he doing, packing fries this late? And he seemed twitchy; then he suddenly said I could go and he'd say no more about it. And I was to keep my mouth shut.

'What am I supposed to keep shut about?' I asked.

Mr Miller raved a little more, like a sad dog who's just had its bone stolen. Then he quietened down and said he was calling the cop and I had better go. I just stood there while he picked up the phone. Then he put it down again.

I suddenly had the feeling I wasn't the only person not supposed to be here. Anyway, he growled and shouted a bit more but I still just stood there. I had a feeling that if the cop came, Mr Miller would have to answer as many questions as I would.

So he told me.

His dad was the 'Shingle Haulage' guy who used to own this land. He sold it to Old Man Visser without knowing the land had been zoned for a factory. Mr Miller said Old Man Visser jacked that up with the local council. The re-zoning would have made the land more valuable.

Just before Old Man Visser died — said Mr Miller — he admitted he'd pulled a double-cross and wanted to put things right. And he said Mr Miller could take a few bagfuls of fries each week to sell and keep the money. He had a deal with some takeaway.

Then Mr Miller said he'd keep some

aside for me each night. He would leave them in the pipe. He said his forewoman was getting suspicious. So I could take the blame but never get caught in the factory. I could be — said Mr Walker — the Fries Phantom. He would tip me off if the local cop came around.

I liked that a lot. And the thought of unlimited fries was like a dream! Now, I know a lot of his story didn't really sound right, but I didn't care. And becoming the Fries Phantom meant I wasn't just the local greenie's kid any more. I was *somebody* — and I was getting back at William Visser, too.

. . .

So that was how I became the Fries Phantom. Then all this hassle blew up over the factory closing. Mr Miller wanted a couple more big deals to go through. But when I went down the tunnel, my usual tub of fries wasn't there.

So I went into the factory. It was dark and

Mr Miller wasn't there. Then the lights suddenly went on and standing there was that old ghost-guy with white hair that everyone had been talking about.

YAAAHHHHH!

That's all I can say for now. Paul Knox (who can be quite bossy) says it will spoil the rest if I tell the ending now. But I am allowed to say two things.

Mr Miller was never seen again.

And I've gone right off fries.

This ends the story of the Fries Phantom and the Great Fries Mystery.

PS Your sister Nicole is much nicer than you. And she's better-looking.

Six

I have to put Nicole's story about Eric the Ear-biter here. Not that I want to, but Nicole hassled me and thinks it is an important link. I suppose the bit about Roller is but that's all.

Please remember any statements made about me are very biased. —P.K.

Nicole Knox

THURSDAY AND SATURDAY: Actually I
think mine's the only really interesting part
and shows what a girl with spunk can do.
I've got lots of that (even if I do say so
myself) and will need it when I'm a pro
sportsperson earning megabucks a year.

I think there's a big future in contact
sports for women; all the boys I've spoken
to agree with me. William Visser said he'd
love to be in contact with me — the creep.

Anyway, I got together this mixed-
gender rugby team. Hadley have one, and a
couple of other towns. I'm going to try it out
but I may change to soccer. It depends a lot
on how many of my bones get broken. Mum
says at least there's no chance of brain-
damage but I'm not quite sure how she
means that. Nothing nice, from the way
Paul laughed.

But not even Paul could laugh when I

got Eric the Ear-biter to come to our school. And Mr Walker was very impressed too, but he did seem a bit funny about it. He's been coaching us and he's OK. But Eric will give us the killer instinct we need.

We have some good players. Jamie-Lee, the Wolf, the Fries Phantom and Tank Bennet, who can trample most kids his age and a lot older. Anyway, I felt we had a good chance. Even the TV people were interested, so it could really lead places. I could become what they call a 'Sporting Icon' at the age of eleven.

Anyway, that evening I made the big announcement, Mum and Mr Walker went off to a Parent–Teacher thing, to discuss the fries closure. I suppose I'd been shutting that out, most kids have. Except William Visser who is big-noting in the most sickening way.

Imogen Visser is better but I've always

thought she was a bit strange, because she likes Paul. Anyway, it started when I asked Paul about his mate, Rick. Rick has dropped right out of sight after school and not even Paul can find him. He's even missed rugby practice and I had to lay it on the line — turn up or dip out. He muttered an excuse and promised he'd show. He'd better.

Well, after dinner, I was getting ready to go out. There was still heaps of light for a practice. I was on the couch, getting my stuff together when I noticed something. A folded news clipping down the side of the cushions. I pulled it out. It was faded yellow and creased — and dated 1968! Ancient history.

Paul saw it. He said Mr Walker dropped some old clippings, it was probably one of those. I chucked it on the table and went to get my boots. When I came back, Paul was reading it. Mr Politically-Correct himself who's always telling me to mind my own business.

I told him that and he mumbled something about newspapers not being private. And he looked really strange, so I asked him what was wrong. He just shook his head, nothing. So I zoomed out and forgot about it.

Practice was great and even Rick turned up.

. . .

So Thursday morning came and it was a great day. I got up early, beat Paul to the bathroom as usual. I put on full school uniform for the special occasion. Mum gasped and asked who was I, and what had I done with her daughter? Ha ha ha. Paul asked if I was trying for the next Mrs Eric Ear-biter, typically lame joke.

I left early and biked the long way to

school, past the headland, for the exercise. The sun was shining, the sea looked really wonderful and I hated the thought of leaving all this. Then, past the headland, I saw something strange.

There's this big patch of native bush with a walkway through it. Some wooden benches where the walkway starts and beside them was Roller. He had half a dozen cages heaped on the benches and was opening them one by one.

He was letting out his budgies!

I stopped. Roller loves budgies but he was letting them go. They were whizzing up in all colours, flying into the bush.

'Hey Roller!' I yelled. 'What're you doing?'

He turned and his little spectacles flashed. He just looked at me and said, 'There's plenty of native stuff for them to eat, they'll be all right'

'Yes, but why are you doing it?'

'Why not?' His spectacles flashed again and he turned back to the last cage.

Well, I always did think he was a bit out to lunch. You know, a sandwich short of a picnic. So I kept going and looked back once. He had opened the last cage and was letting them fly away.

Definitely weird.

. . .

And talking about weird things (apart from Paul who was born that way) Mr Walker was in a funny mood all through morning class. I felt we should be discussing Eric's visit and how brilliant of me to arrange it. He said it was just a visit and wouldn't teach us anything.

I noticed something else. I had pinned up a lot of stuff about how good a player Eric was. He pinned up stuff about Eric biting people and getting banned. I wondered about that — jealous?

Anyway we were all burning because celebrities don't often come this way. He was due at mid-morning break, ten thirty.

But ten thirty came and went. Ten thirty-five. Ten forty. Then the bell went for the end of break and I could not believe it! Eric hadn't shown!

Mr Walker said he wasn't coming, probably too many appointments. So most of the kids were trailing inside again. I ducked around the back of the school in case he was on the wrong road. Then I heard this car.

It was a big four-wheel drive turning into the road. People often get the turn-off mixed up. It came slowly and stopped. I heard voices.

FIRST VOICE: (male): This place? Looks more like a cowshed.

SECOND VOICE: (female) There's only one school this end of nowhere. Has to be it.

VOICE THREE: (who was Eric) Can we get on with this crap?

The car doors opened and shut. I looked around the hedge by the gate. Three people got out and one seemed unsteady. He nearly fell into the ditch by the roadside.

Voice One was a cool guy, chinos and a baggy yellow shirt, bleached hair and shades.

Voice Two looked just as cool — young woman in black T-shirt with 'Moscow Circus' lettered on it and baggy green shorts. Her hair was up in lilac spikes.

Eric was Voice Three. He looked as solid as a chunk of red-faced concrete. He did sway a bit though, when he walked, and his voice sounded like wheels over gravel.

'Any chance of a drink?'

'No,' said Lilac-Spikes.

'Behave, Eric,' said Shades.

'Hey!' I yelled, erupting from the hedge. 'You can have coffee or fruit juice!'

They all jumped and Eric nearly fell into the roadside ditch. Lilac-Spikes was first to recover. 'Great, kid! Lead on!'

Ms Appleyard had come out looking for me. Her mouth fell open when she saw the three of them and she took a long hard look at Eric. She hauled them off to the staff-room for coffee and I told Mr Walker.

He gave us a bit of a lecture, as usual. No questions about ear-biting or dirty tricks. Or what he earned, or about the three marriages.

So Eric came in. He still had a cup of coffee with him and his face was less red. He began speaking slowly and Lilac-Spikes came in at the end of each sentence. 'Eric says this —' and 'Eric quantifies —' Whoever heard of 'quantifies'? She had a bright smile on her face and a rather screechy voice.

Mr Walker sat at his desk, looking blank. Ms Appleyard yawned quite a bit, and I sat there, a bit puzzled. I mean he talked about his matches, what he did as a kid, on tour, but nothing actually about the game.

He reached the end and Lilac-Spikes said, gee, she wished there was time for questions. I jumped up and shouted that I had a question about rugby. And from the back of the room, Mr Walker said we hadn't heard much about that — rather nastily I thought.

'Sure thing, honey,' said Lilac-Spikes with a bright smile.

'OK,' said Eric.

We all hushed. Eric was awesome. Not just because he bit off ears, either. He once scored a try with six guys hanging onto him. He was two-legged carnage and a one-man scrum. He opened his mouth.

'Always keep your eye on the ball,' he said.

That was it and we looked at each other. We were open–mouthed and awe-struck at those simple words. Winning was as easy as that. Keep your eye on the ball.

Eric went, after that. Me and Mr Walker went as far as the gate with them. Eric shook my hand and said I was a nice kid. Lilac-Spikes beamed at us like a tooth-paste ad. Eric said he wanted to drive and Shades said no. They reversed up the road, turned at the top and drove off.

'Magic,' I said.

Mr Walker said nothing.

. . .

Saturday morning. The match. Brother Paul (who wants all the best bits for himself) said I don't have to talk about the Great Potato Fight on Friday or anything else. I don't mind. As far as I'm concerned, the rugby match against Hadley was just as important.

It was a total massacre. We all lined up, remembering what Eric had said. The whistle blew and we charged forward. Massacre — we flattened them! I scored twice and so did Rick. Wolf did a fantastic drop-kick just before half-time and next half it was the same. We went over them like a steam-roller and they're a much bigger school. The Fries Phantom seemed a bit out to it and got a stern word from me.

So we all came off the field and our side was cheering. (And I did notice you weren't there, brother, despite your promise.) And Mr Walker had a BIG SMILE.

The Hadley Principal, Ms Price, did not. She knew that Eric the Ear-biter had come to our school and she accused Mr Walker of unfair tactics! In fact, she said <u>terror</u>-tactics. She said her team were just about holding onto their ears all through the match.

Mr Walker snapped back. He said her team was sloppy and over-confident. He said Eric the Ear-biter was no help at all. Ms Price sneered at that. She made it sound like Mr Walker had offered ten bucks for every ear we got.

Now <u>that</u> was crazy. If Mr Walker was that generous, I would have come off with a sackful of them. They went off, snarling at each other like a pair of dogs.

He came back up to us when we'd changed. He handed out candy bars and said 'great job'. But he was tight-lipped like he had something on his mind.

'Listen,' he said. 'How come you never played that well before?'

'We kept our eye on the ball like Eric said,' replied Jamie-Lee.

We all nodded, it was simple as that. Mr Walker seemed like he was biting his lip. Then he said, 'That is just about the most basic rule of rugby. I must've told you a hundred times. So how come you never listened to me?'

'Mr Walker,' said the Fries Phantom patiently, because sometimes you have to spell things out for adults, 'you're not Eric the Ear-biter.'

Mr Walker looked like he was going to bite his tongue off for a moment. Then he sighed, shook his head and muttered another 'well done'.

(And then of course, YOU had to make a dramatic entrance, Paul Knox, like the world was going to explode! And drag him out then race off with him. And you promised to come to the match!

And what about those choppers and the cops coming. I am waiting for an explanation and will make sure I get it!)

Anyway to finish my story, the other big piece of news was that the Fries Phantom said he would never eat fries again. I was going to shout the whole team (a week's pocket-money) and he just produced a carrot and two sticks of celery!

And (to really finish) during the match, I got tackled by two Hadley forwards who made Roller look slim. So I think I might try soccer. At least I'll keep both my ears.

NOTE TO PAUL: This is going to be the only really interesting part of the book, you do realise that, don't you? And will anyone ever be allowed to read the FAMOUS LAST CHAPTERS.

Yours waiting (probably forever),
NICOLE

Seven

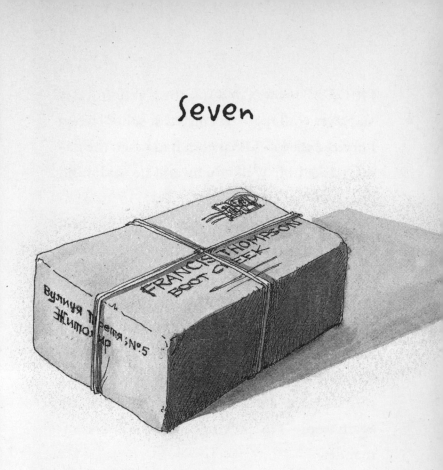

UPDATE: *I had to think long and hard before writing these next few chapters. The Great Potato Fight is OK, but not what followed. And I suppose the two are linked.*

I will never know how much the potatoes triggered off Roller. The last straw? — P.K.

FRIDAY: This was going to be a very full day and a very full night. It started at school when I noticed the Fries Phantom had taken the day off. I asked Mr Walker why and he said mind your own business.

Yes, and I should talk about my best mate Rick, who I have hardly mentioned so far.

Rick is a nice guy with short brown hair who wants to join the army and become a weapons-master. He may sound really aggressive but he's not. Last year it was a space shuttle pilot and he will change his mind again soon. I'm picking a submarine commander.

I also have to talk about the four Visser sons. Cornelis, Dirck, Pieter and Jacob. Cornelis is up himself and his son is William — also up himself. Pieter's daughter is Imogen, who is beautiful, and Dirck's daughter is Leila, who is a pain. None of them had more than one kid and Jacob never married.

They each grow a different brand of potato. Rembrandt Yellow, Mosby Brown, Trompe and, lastly, One-eyed Jack. Each is convinced he grows the best potatoes and they hate each other. Each is convinced he got ripped off when the estate was divided up. Cornelis and Pieter voted for the factory closure and Dirck and Jacob against.

It all started when school had finished for the day.

Friday is when the four Visser brothers deliver potatoes to the factory. They don't like each other and Mr Miller would arrange for them to come at different times. But he'd suddenly left town, leaving no forwarding address and Mum was in charge.

She must have forgotten because all four came at the same time. I was in town at the time and saw at once there was going to be trouble.

Mum was looking pretty hassled like she had something on her mind. She was arranging who could unload first and chose Pieter, since he was nearest. Jacob objected loudly, saying Pieter had voted for closure and, anyway, his potatoes tasted like old socks boiled in flour.

Pieter shouted that Jacob grew One-eyed Jacks; they were only fit for pigs and people with no taste.

Dirck shouted that only his Rembrandt Yellows were used and the others probably ended up as landfill.

Cornelis (who grew Trompes) yelled that they had better all remember who won the award.

Well, he did, and has never let his brothers forget it. He even had the medal painted on the side of his car. Anyway, the words were scarcely out of his mouth when a Rembrandt Yellow bounced off his head.

Dirck didn't throw it. None of the brothers did but next minute the air was full of potatoes. And all the people around, including most of the factory women, joined in. I think everyone was just too stressed.

Russell's dad was there and tried to stop it. A Mosby Brown hit him, then two well-aimed Rembrandts. He went cross-eyed and staggered back to his car. Then came the tinkle of broken glass as a nearby shop window went. And the shatter of windscreen glass as the trucks were hit.

There were potatoes flying everywhere. A Trompe sailed past my head, a Rembrandt Yellow bounced off and I ducked two One-eyed Jacks. And looked up, just in time to see something.

Roller was cycling into town. And only Roller could be quite unaware of what was happening. He was only interested in himself. Anyway a potato hit him, then another. He wobbled, more potatoes hit him and he crashed down. His bag burst open, scattering what was inside.

There was a shout of laughter as Roller tumbled over. I told you nobody likes him. And the potatoes were already flying again when Cornelis was suddenly knocked off his truck by a jet of water. Then Pieter and Dirck. Not Jacob because two well-aimed Trompes had already knocked him off.

Mum and two others had come out with the factory firehose and swung it around at anyone holding a potato. Roller chose that moment to stand up and copped the full force. I was not throwing anything and got soaked too — my heartless mother thought this was amusing when I told her.

They turned off the hose. Roller was picking up the stuff out of his bag. Letters mostly. I went to help but he stuffed them in and looked around. He was dripping wet, and mud-stained, but there was a funny superior look on his face. Like he knew something that we didn't. Then he cycled off down the street. The brothers had scrambled to their feet again, Pieter was actually reaching for a Trompe when another voice cut across everything.

'Stop this! Everything stop! You are stupid boys, I knew this would happen.'

And out of the factory stalked an old man in a long black coat. He had white hair and a long white beard. Hendrick Visser — and he was no ghost either!

'Put down those spuds and come in here,' he shouted. Mr Visser always called potatoes 'spuds'. He still had a Dutch accent too, after fifty years. 'All the rest of you — go!'

And everyone did. Except for Constable Pearson and the four Visser sons who suddenly looked like scared little boys. They exchanged looks and followed their father into the factory. Mum saw me and came across.

'Go on and get out of those wet clothes,' she said. 'Explanations later — go on.'

I went on down the street. Roller had stopped by the mail-box and was stuffing the letters inside. Some were mud-stained, but he didn't seem to care. A couple had dropped and I picked them up. They were addressed to newspapers. Roller grabbed them and put them in the box.

'Who're you writing all that stuff to?' I asked.

Roller didn't answer. He cleaned his glasses on his wet T-shirt and I felt sorry for him. It seemed like nothing good ever happened to Roller.

'I can get you a towel at our place,' I said.

He just shook his head and got on his bike again. He wheeled off a bit then stopped.

Then he came back and pulled twenty bucks from his pocket.

'Paul, you know that little electronic place at Hadley. They're holding a parcel for me. Will you get it tomorrow?'

'Saturday?' It was Nicole's match and I was looking forward to seeing her get jumped on by the other team.

'Yeah, got to be tomorrow.' His face was still blank. 'Only five bucks, you can keep the rest.' As he went, he looked back. His spectacles flashed again. 'Buy yourself some fries.'

And there was just something strange about the way he said those last four words. Like he was laughing at a joke nobody else knew. He swung his bike around and went off.

Why not? I thought. Twenty bucks is twenty bucks — well fifteen bucks.

I got on my own bike. I was only halfway home when someone called me. It was Rick, peeping over a hedge and looking scared. And never mind me being wet, he wanted to see me straight away. At his place.

'I didn't think there'd be so many people at the meeting,' he said. 'The factory was supposed to be closed.' He looked really scared. 'I wanted it to look like an act of ghostly revenge.'

'The gravestones? You?'

He nodded, still scared. 'I just wanted to shock everyone.'

'You did that all right,' I said.

'It was supposed to look like an act of supernatural revenge and sort of shock them …?'

'It shocked them all right,' I said.

Rick's house is on the ridge overlooking the town. His dad is farm manager for Pieter Visser. Rick led me around to the side and showed me something.

'It's a trebuchet,' he said, pronouncing it 'traybooshay'.

A trebuchet is a siege engine that was used against castles before cannon were invented. It worked on weights and counter-weights and I don't want to say too much about it. Except that it worked really well and was a lot more accurate than Rick thought.

He'd been making it as a class project when all this fries thing blew up. And he had the bright idea of trying to scare people with the ghostly wrath of Old Man Visser. So he pinched the gravestones one night — making four trips to get them — and, as they say, the rest you know.

Anyway, his siege engine had one final use. When we chopped it up, the fire dried my clothes nicely. I pointed out to Rick that he might've spent twenty years in jail if he'd killed anyone and made him promise never to make another one.

I did feel a bit mean saying that.

Considering I knew about a criminal on the run from the cops. Considering that made me what they call 'an accessory', which means I might be doing hard time in jail.

First though, I'd better finish off explaining why Old Man Visser came back from the grave.

. . .

Mum got me, Nicole and Mr Walker together that evening.

Of course, Hendrick Vissser was not back from the grave. In fact he was never in it.

You see (Mum said) Hendrick Visser had a dream about spending the last years of his life on a Pacific island. He wanted to be the oldest beach-comber in the world.

But he also knew his sons would never leave him alone. Also that sooner or later, they would fight over Visser Fries. So, he arranged his 'death' (swept away in the flooding creek) but set up the family trust first. The trustees didn't know he was still alive until he pounced on them.

That time in the cemetery, he was just looking at his own grave when Russell Pearson came by. He didn't mean to scare Russell quite that much — was just about to ask him about the missing gravestones.

'That mystery,' said Mum, 'will never be solved.'

I kept a straight face, which wasn't difficult. I had worries too, and they got worse every time I glanced at Mr Walker.

And that stuff about Mr Miller being allowed to take fries. All nonsense. Mum had guessed what was going on. Not even the Fries Phantom could have eaten all those fries. So Hendrick Visser paid Mr Miller a surprise visit.

Ir surprised the Phantom too. It's put him off fries for life.

That was why the four Visser brothers all arrived at the same time. He had arranged with Mum to get them together, tell them off and disappear back to his island.

'He loves it there,' said Mum. 'Nothing to do but fish all day and eat coconuts. There's bananas there too, and he's opened a little banana-chips bar.'

Old habits die hard.

'One thing,' said Mr Walker. He'd been listening to all this in silence. 'When did Hendrick Visser tell you?'

Mum was silent a moment and actually looked embarrassed. Then she admitted she'd always known. She was the one person Old Man Visser told, so when the fries thing started, she told him. Even beach-combers have mobile phones.

'One other thing,' said Mr Walker. 'Why did he tell you?'

Mum went a little pink at that. Then she

sighed and admitted that Hendrick Visser had asked her to go with him. Even to bring us kids and get married. He'd always had a secret thing for Mum.

Mr Walker was looking at her like he'd never seen her before. So were we. Our mum had known all this time and said nothing! Nicole broke the silence.

'You mean, Mum — we could have been adopted by a millionaire and grown up on a Pacific island?'

I nearly felt sorry for Mr Walker when she said that. Nearly. Mum just got cross and said it was her decision and what if a shark had eaten Nicole? I said the shark would have sicked her back up again and Mum ordered us both to bed. I had one more question.

'Mum, who threw that potato at Cornelis and started the fight. Did you see?'

'Obviously someone who didn't like Cornelis,' she said and went pink again.

I didn't mind going to bed. I still had an awful lot to think about even if the fries factory was safe again. The jobs safe, the town and school safe. Everyone safe except us.

Mum should have married Mr Visser. Even if Nicole did get eaten by a shark. Because instead of that, she'd married Mr Walker. And he was thirty years on the run from the cops.

I didn't sleep much that night.

Eight

These last three chapters are mine, too. It's funny to take three chapters to write this because it all happened so quickly. Like in a few hours and just when we thought all our troubles were over. — P.K.

SATURDAY: Before I can talk about Saturday, I have to talk about Thursday. Thursday evening when Nicole found that news clipping down the side of the couch.

I opened it. I didn't think a newspaper was sort of personal. And I was wondering why Mr Walker snapped at me, the way he did. The paper was yellow, the date was December 1968 and it was titled 'WHERE ARE THEY NOW?'

It was a big article that covered half the page. A photo of a wrecked building, and smaller ones of people. The wrecked building had an X and a caption, '*Where body was found*'.

There was a lot of trouble in the late nineteen-sixties with student 'activists' or 'radicals'. They were protesting about a war in Vietnam, things at home — or just protesting. And some of them used bombs.

They blew things up. Not people, just what they called 'symbols of oppression'.

Banks and court buildings and government departments. One person was killed, an old guy who lived on the street and had gone to sleep in the doorway of a bank.

One group was the worst. They called themselves 'Red Guard' and they bombed about six places, including the bank where the old street-guy died. They were trained in Libya and knew all about bombs.

Anyway, four were caught in a police raid and two escaped. A man and a woman, both about twenty years old. They had code-names; she was ROSA and he was KROTO, and they were the two worst. Both escaped and were still on the run.

There were photos of them both. They had angry faces with somehow hurt eyes. The woman had a sharp nose and chin, the man had long hair. And he had little pointed ears; it was the ears I noticed first.

Mr Walker had ears just like them. He

had a habit of fiddling with one ear when he was reading a book. And although it was about thirty years ago, the rest of the photo looked like him, too. Except for the long hair.

But was it him? Or a brother, or a cousin? And thinking about that, I was remembering he never talked about himself, or where he came from. But could it really be *our* Mr Walker? He was so quiet and so — boring. He was so much a typical school-teacher that they could have cloned him.

He and Nicole would be back soon from practice. So what to do? I couldn't just say, 'Hi, Kroto, blown up any banks lately?' I still wasn't sure it *was* him. I had to talk to Mum first and she had enough problems right now.

It's waited thirty years I thought, it can wait a day or two longer. I hid the clipping in a safe place. I read somewhere that really skilled bombers can make explosives from all kinds of stuff. If he suspected, all he had to do was mix some detergent with floor-cleaner maybe, add some disinfectant and — bang. There'd be nothing left of us but a hole in the ground.

I decided to talk to Mum about it. I wasn't really sure and it could wait until the weekend. Saturday, after the match.

But something else happened Saturday, after the match.

. . .

I was actually feeling OK on Saturday. I'd told myself it was crazy and maybe he was a reformed character. Or maybe it was a twin brother. And Mum's not stupid, *she* must've seen something in him.

And I had that little job to do with Roller.

But the more I thought about it, the more I realised I couldn't. And not because I

wanted to watch Nicole maybe biting someone's ear off. But this was too important and
Roller would have to get his own package. Or
maybe I could do it on Monday. It wouldn't
hurt to ask him.

When the others left, I was going to
follow on my bike. I kept looking at Mr
Walker and thinking, no way, he's so *ordinary*!
Anyway they left and I just mucked around a
little. I looked at the clipping again — after all
this time, would the cops still be looking?

I phoned Roller and got no answer. I
knew his parents were away — they often just
went off and left him. I thought I'd rather
have an ex-bomber for a step-dad than a
mother and father like that. They were
designer people and poor Roller wasn't a
designer kid.

And I thought about Roller, remembering the way he looked at everyone. And that
strange tone of voice — *buy yourself some fries*.

And the headshaking, I had to *do it this morning*.

I tried his phone again. No answer. I glanced at my watch and flipped — nearly an hour had passed. Nicole would never believe I just forgot. I grabbed my bike and wheeled out onto the road. I was just in time to see him.

Our road cuts into another that leads out of town. It comes down from the ridge where some really nice homes overlook the sea. Roller's mum and dad live there. And he was biking down the road.

So he was home and didn't answer the phone. Well, that's Roller, and at least I could tell him now. Then I stopped because I would never get to him on time.

Roller was pedalling as fast as he could. His knees worked up and down like pistons, his big body crouched over the bike and his spectacle-flashing eyes staring straight ahead.

I yelled, but he didn't hear me. He took the fork that led to the motorway. By the time I got to the end of the road, he was out of sight.

I had never seen Roller move so fast.

OK, so the town oddball was biking fast, for once. I don't know why I felt something was wrong. It was just a tingle in me — maybe my crazy imagination going into over-drive.

Letting his budgies go? Looking a bit strange? Well he always did. And his words kept popping back into my mind like fries sizzling in hot fat.

'Buy yourself some fries!'

I still had his money and I could make the end of the match if I moved fast. Roller might want that packet, so I'd better tell him I couldn't do it. Leave a note and the money at the door.

Roller's parents had a really classy split-level place with lots of patio. One of those landscape places in the glossy magazines. And it still looked neat, nice and ordinary, except for one thing — the mailbox. It was packed with mail and overflowing, scattering over the ground. There were bootmarks where Roller had walked over it.

Why suddenly lose interest in clearing the mail? His parents would freak, and Roller was afraid of them. Not my business, I thought and biked up to the door. I would leave a note under the doormat.

A breeze came and the door creaked. Then it swung gently open.

Not clearing the mail? Leaving the door unlocked?

From the door, I could see through to the kitchen and main living area. There was a funny stale smell in the air and I could see why. The kitchen was cluttered with takeaway boxes from Mr Trangs Red Dragon café. Some on the floor and squashed flat, others on the bench. Plates were littering the table, one broken on the floor.

He was going to leave all this for his parents to find. The word around town was they were looking for an excuse to kick him out. This would be it.

And then I heard the noise.

It was a faint fluttery noise like tiny fingernails scratching. There were stairs leading down to the basement and an open door. The noise came from there. Roller's room. Jamie-Lee, whose dad does the gardening, says Roller has the whole basement.

Then I heard another noise. A loud 'click'.

I had no reason to go inside. I had no reason to go to the top of the stairs and listen. Or to walk down them. I still don't know why I did. It was just that tingle, that sense of something wrong — *wrong*.

The basement light was on. Looking up,

the hall light was on. I think the kitchen one was too. As though Roller had just done what he liked and not cared any more.

The fluttering scratchy noise was louder. It was coming from inside the basement, sounding like unseen demons were waiting. Like some scaly-clawed thing was waiting to pounce. So I pushed the door open.

Roller's room was painted different colours in crazy angles. They zig-zagged black, yellow and red. Big staring mouths of pop stars and laser prints of his budgies. Eco-posters and fantasy art. And along one side, the full awesome bank of Roller's computer base.

Looking at the room, I realised just how different he was from his parents. This was like some kind of escape place from the real world.

How far to Davistown, Paul? Was that where he was headed?

The fluttery noise came from a tape-deck — the noise from a blank tape. And, as I watched, it clicked and began to rewind. There were papers and envelopes scattered around it on the table. I picked up a list — addresses. To his parents in the city, the newspapers, even the police.

I heard another 'click' from somewhere.

My foot nudged something and I looked down. I picked it up, a small lead box with the top ripped up. On the table was some wrapping paper with Ukraine stamps on it.

The tape finished rewinding and I pressed 'play'.

I remember Roller posting all those letters and packets.

The screen flickered into life. Roller. He was sitting in front of a video camera, dressed in black, his shoulders hunched, spectacles flashing. His fat chin wobbled as he spoke.

'I hate the world and have no place in it. That is why I am doing this.'

He fidgeted around in the chair and his spectacles flashed again. And I felt an awful creepy feeling come over me, like I knew what he was going to say.

'I hate the god, Money. I hate being a freak to everyone. I hate my parents because they treat me like I'm a zero. They're going to chuck me out. All they care about is money. All this town cares about is money and the stupid fries place.'

This was unreal. His voice whispered and stumbled, he swallowed. A little down from the tape-deck was a work-bench, cluttered with tools, wire and strange bits of equipment. In the middle was a square metal box, the size of a small suitcase.

Another 'click'.

It came from the metal box. I opened the lid.

'Now I'll show this town and the whole world

that I'm somebody. Everyone will know my name, more than any other person. They call me Roller but I'll roll over them all …'

He gave a little giggle then kept on talking. About commerce and greed and how people treated him. But I wasn't listening because a creepy feeling was crawling over my skin like icy caterpillars. I just looked at the thing in the box.

It had two thick coils and a long silver cylinder with yellow clamps at both ends. They were just the main bits, but it was the cylinder I was looking at. There were foreign words like Russian printing and a big red sign stencilled on it. It was the sign that made my skin crawl.

Mr Walker was Civil Defence Warden and I had seen that sign when he lectured the class.

Radiation. The cylinder held radioactive material. Roller was still speaking behind me.

'My device will wipe this town off the map.'

And I'm looking at this thing. A whole tangle of different-coloured wires like worms. And a timer looking like it was made from a digital alarm-clock. It was flashing 'twenty-six'.

'My device, my nuclear bomb ...'

Roller had made a nuclear bomb.

And it would go off in twenty-six minutes.

Click!

Twenty-five minutes.

Nine

I'd seen something on TV last year about two American kids making a nuclear bomb. Mr Walker was very interested — well he would be. But the FBI grabbed them. They were clever and they'd got all the parts.

Roller was very clever.

I don't know how long I stood looking at it. As though nothing else in the world was real. The TV screen became static again and the tape whirred as it rewound. Master-tape for those copies he posted. Through my horror came another noise.

Click! Twenty-four minutes.

And even then, like I was rooted to the floor. Thinking who I could call. The cops would be too busy laughing; it would take all the twenty minutes to convince them. Or the Army, and *who* to even ask? Or Civil Defence — Mr Walker.

Click! Twenty-three minutes.

Mr Walker. If he was Kroto the Bomber, he might know. Maybe all bombs worked the same way. The two coils looked up at me like horrible goggle eyes. I felt if it clicked again, I'd go mad.

So I was out of that place, running hard, slamming the door behind me and grabbing my bike. Speeding downhill, nearly colliding with a milk truck, the loud angry honk of his horn. It was about ten minutes to the playing field. I did it in six.

The game was over, people gathered back at the school. From all the sulks on Hadley faces, I guessed who had won. There were a lot of people in one of the classrooms. I charged in. The door flung back against the wall, glass breaking.

'Paul Knox, you are in so much trouble,' snapped Ms Appleyard.

Wrong crowd! I turned, ignoring her yell, into the other classroom. The team was there, finished dressing, eating candy bars. Nicole glared at me (for missing the match) but I had no time for her. I could still hear that 'click'.

'Paul?' asked Mr Walker.

'Outside!' I gasped, then in a low voice, 'Kroto.'

It *was* him. I saw the sudden shocked

look in his eyes. Then Ms Appleyard, breathing fire, was storming in after us. Mr Walker, already recovered, told her he'd handle it, pulled me outside.

I don't remember how I told him. I stumbled and gasped, I felt so scared and desperate. I think it was that and the look on my face that told him more. He nodded, pulled me towards his car, the whole school watching as we drove off.

I had time to tell him more on the way. He just nodded then asked, 'How did you know that name?'

I told him.

Then, 'Have you told anyone else?'

'No.'

Just for a horrible moment I wondered if I should have said that. Maybe *he* showed Roller how ... no, crazy thought. We stopped at the house and I ran back up the path. I wrenched the door-handle.

Nothing! I'd slammed it on the way out — locked!

'Are you quite sure about all this?' asked Mr Walker behind me. 'Or is this a dramatic way of telling me you know about my past?'

I had no time for this! There were flowerpots on the porch. I grabbed one and smashed it through the narrow glass pane by the door. I stuck my hand through and turned the door-knob.

Mr Walker just looked at me, my hand running with blood. That and the glass being smashed made him realise how serious I was. So there were no more arguments as he followed me inside. I ran down the steps into the basement and that awful sound came as I did.

Click!

'There!' I pointed.

Mr Walker went over and I followed. He looked at the device and I looked at the read-out. Eleven minutes!

I was still hoping against hope that this was all a sick joke of Roller's. But as Mr Walker looked at the thing, his face went a horrible pale colour; for the first time I saw him look really scared.

He gulped, shook his head slightly then bent over it. Ran a finger along the cylinder — I would not have dared touch it — and the writing. 'Cyrillic script, Russian,' he muttered, 'maybe from one of the new states ...'

'Can you do anything? Disconnect something ... cut it?'

He shook his head. 'Cut what? A short-circuit might just trigger it.'

'What can you do then?'

'Nothing,' he said quietly. 'I wouldn't know how to disarm this.' He shook his head. 'I've heard about these things, they're very unstable. Might blow up anyway.'

'It's going to blow up in ten minutes!'

Click! Nine minutes.

'Then get in the car, warn as many people as we can —'

'Nobody's going anywhere Paul, not in time.'

He began searching the papers on Roller's desk. Maybe there was a manual or diagram of some sort. *Click!* I helped him, then he cursed softly and lifted a metal wastepaper bin. There was a charred mass of papers inside.

'He must have burned everything.'

Click.

Seven minutes! And the horrible goggle eyes of those red coils looking up at us. And I was scared as hell because in a few minutes we just would not exist. Mr Walker was running his hands through his hair, looking around.

'You can do it, Mr Walker,' I said, not believing how steady my voice sounded. 'Roller is seventeen and flunked school. OK, he's clever but no atomic scientist. He must've taken short-cuts and you know about timers and detonators — what did they teach you in Libya?'

'I was never in Libya,' he snapped. 'The cops made that up.'

'Rosa?'

'Police undercover agent. Shut up!'

He was watching the bomb, trying to remember everything he knew. And with such a curious hurt look in his eyes, as though reliving those times — the dead street-guy ...

Click! Six minutes.

'Two parts of this come together and form a critical mass,' he whispered. 'But something has to kick it off.'

And the red coil-eyes goggled up, saying: *no, you can't win; soon the white-hot breath of destruction will reduce you to cindered molecules. I am going to win in a hot awesome blast —*

'Did you notice anything Paul — anything about the place when you came in?'

'No. It was all dirty and the lights were on, then I heard —'

Five minutes!

Mr Walker shushed me, looking around, 'The light was on when you came in?'

'Yes.'

'Wait here.'

And he was gone, running up the stairs. Another click, four minutes, and something really horrible happened. Instead of clicking each minute, the digital read-out began to run down in seconds. Like it was in a hurry to end things, the red lights flashing, the digital figures scrambling like little spiky demons, anxious to be causing death.

I could hear Mr Walker upstairs, opening cupboards, kicking things over, hunting for something.

The numbers chasing down into two minutes, one minute.

Thirty seconds. Twenty seconds. Ten seconds —

I shut my eyes. It was like hot black breath was hissing around me. A long black ten seconds, blacker and blacker. Then I opened my eyes again — and it was still black.

Had it happened? Was this what death was like? Just utter darkness to wander in forever? But still a sense — a smell — that I was in Roller's basement. Or had I just taken that impression with me? And in the darkness, footsteps and a light — and a voice.

'You were right about the short-cuts.'

A match flared into healthy yellow flame, touched to one of the candles in those wall-brackets by the door. It threw out a dim soft light as he came up. He held the candle down to the blank readout. The red-coil eyes goggled up in angry frustration.

'Don't even think about touching it,' said Mr Walker.

I wasn't even thinking about it. 'What did you do?'

He sighed. 'Roller leaving the lights on made me think about power. And that.'

He pointed. 'That' was a thick electric cord, connected to the tin box and running to a hole in the wall.

'What …?'

He touched my shoulder and smiled. A trembly smile, though. 'Short-cuts. Roller used electric power to generate the charge. Clumsy, but he'd never have the know-how for a proper detonator. So that was it.'

I must've sounded very dense. 'What was it?'

'I turned him off at the mains.'

He pushed the candle into my hands. Hot wax ran down onto my fingers but I didn't mind. It was a reminder that I was still alive. Mr Walker pulled out his mobile phone.

'Now let's see who we can get interested.'

Roller's device was dark and silent. Beside me, Mr Walker began to speak urgently into his phone.

Ten

Mr Walker called someone in Civil Defence. Then he had to call someone else. And someone else. And half an hour later, more choppers than I had ever seen began arriving. And an hour later, more sirens than I had ever heard came screaming down the road. Roller's house was surrounded with red flashing lights and blue uniforms.

There were yellow tapes on both ends of the street. Everyone in town was gaping behind them. Six army guys spent two hours in Roller's house and came out with Roller's device in two parts. They handled them like they were made of glass.

We watched as they did this. The cops had politely asked us not to go anywhere. Six big cops stood around us to make sure we didn't. The two pieces were put into the back of a van, packed in lots of foam rubber. Then it drove off with cop-cars and army jeeps around it. It drove very slowly indeed.

'Remember, I haven't told anyone about you-know-who,' I whispered to Mr Walker.

'You don't have to. I will,' he replied.

'Don't be crazy! You don't have to!' I nearly yelled.

He just smiled. 'Yes, I do, Paul. I've lived

with it long enough. I want closure.'

There was a really senior cop there, with lots of silver flashing on his shoulder-tabs. Mr Walker went up to him, they talked a minute and the cop's eyes went round. A couple of other cops took me aside and got a statement. Then I was driven home.

Mr Walker was taken off in another car.

Another senior cop came with me, also with lots of silver on his shoulders. He got me and Mum together (Nicole was sent outside, much to her fury) and he told her what had happened. He said I'd been very brave, which made me wriggle a bit. Then he explained, very nicely, that Mr Walker was helping them with their inquiries.

Then he left. Mum just sat there — even though Nicole was rapping on the window and loudly demanding to be let in. I told her everything again and she said she wished I'd come to her. I felt really bad because I realised for the first time, how much she loved him. Then she hugged me and said I *was* very brave.

The cop had said tell nobody and that included Nicole. She was truly disgusted when Mum let her back in, practically accused me of creating the whole thing to ruin her special day. She never forgets and she'll get me for it one day.

And that was nearly the end of my story.

• • •

Roller had put on a hairpiece and dark glasses and enrolled in a crash slimming course. He'd even set up some fake ID and cleaned out his parents' bank account. Now he's in a 'secure home' somewhere. Chances are he'll be there a long time.

I know what he planned to do was terrible, but I still almost feel sorry for him. He did try and pay me back for treating him like a person; he was just very twisted and lonely.

And there must be other Rollers in this world.

Like those American kids, he got most of what he wanted off the Internet; the radioactive stuff came from the Ukraine. Roller had spent two years building it, getting the parts machined, and everything. His parents lived overhead and never knew a thing.

The cops and an army guy paid us one more visit. They said we could never *ever* talk about it. Yes, and they said it would never have gone off. In fact they said that a little too much. But Roller used the Internet like a spider who knew every black website. And *he* thought it would.

The radiation would have taken a quarter of a million years to go away.

Roller's house is on the market; his parents never came back.

But Mr Walker did. The next day!

• • •

I will never know why the cops released him. But I can make a pretty good guess. Mum took the cop and the army guy aside and I think she laid it on the line. Mr Walker back or a major media blow-up. And prosecuting the guy who saved a whole town from nuclear disaster? Wouldn't they look great?

Maybe they were thinking along the same lines. But he did come back and for the first time in my life, I was pleased to see him.

• • •

Nicole is tossing up between pro golf and soccer. She wants to make her first million before she's twenty; the scary thing is, she probably will.

The Fries Phantom was promised all the fries he could eat by Mr Visser. But he wasn't a phantom legend any more; he discovered that only stolen fries tasted that good. Now he's into health food and thinks anyone who eats takeaways is a Sybarite.

Russell Splatter-mode Pearson went back to his mum but we still e-mail and will meet up when I go to the city.

Sarah Lucas doesn't like the city. But both her mum and dad have jobs there now. Not all stories can have a happy ending.

Hendrick Visser went back to his Pacific island. He very wisely did not tell his sons which one. I hope his empty grave goes on waiting for him a long time.

• • •

So all the fuss died away. The story went around town that Roller made up a bomb scare, then had a nervous breakdown. The cops must have moved very fast to round up those letters and video-packets before they could be delivered.

And the day Mr Walker came back, we

went for a walk. He brought his little brown satchel along with him.

We went a bit inland where there's a sort of salt-water lake. A lot of birds stalking around the shores or flying overhead. Mangrove trees, whose roots held the mud like big-knuckled fingers. We sat there in silence a little time.

I said maybe we could have stopped Roller by treating him better, by listening to him. Mr Walker said that when you don't listen, some people get desperate. I think he was talking about himself, back in the sixties.

Then he asked me to call him Stephen. I said, 'OK … Stephen.'

He said he was glad he had married Mum. And he was very pleased she didn't marry Hendrick Visser. He said I should be pleased too. I asked him why.

He said he couldn't help noticing I rather liked Imogen Visser. And that she rather liked me. He said that might lead to something in due course. But if my mum had married Hendrick Visser then Imogen and me would be related.

And (he said) if you're related, you couldn't have any kind of a relationship.

'Thanks for telling me that, Stephen,' I replied, and smiled.

I had to smile. It was a pretty weak joke. But it was the first one he ever made.